An Old Ukrainian Folktale

the Mitten

Retold by Alvin Tresselt

Illustrations by Yaroslava

Adapted from the version by E. Rachev

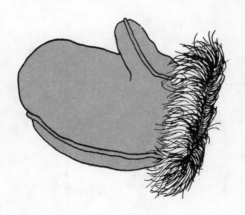

SCHOLASTIC BOOK SERVICES
NEW YORK · TORONTO · LONDON · AUCKLAND · SYDNEY · TOKYO

W9-AXP-114

For Niki

No part of this publication may be reproduced in whole or in part, or stored in a retrieval system, or transmitted in any form or by any means, electronic, mechanical, photocopying, recording, or otherwise, without written permission of the publisher. For information regarding permission, write to Lothrop Lee & Shepard Co., Inc., a division of William Morrow & Co., Inc., 105 Madison Avenue, New York, N.Y. 10016.

ISBN 0-590-32293-1

Copyright © 1964 by Lothrop, Lee & Shepard. All rights reserved. This edition is published by Scholastic Book Services, a division of Scholastic Inc., 50 West 44th Street, New York, N.Y. 10036, by arrangement with Lothrop, Lee & Shepard Co., Inc.

12 11 10 9 8 7 6 5 4 3 2 1   02   2 3 4 5 6/8
Printed in the U.S.A.   18

The Mitten

It was the coldest day of the winter,
and a little boy was trudging through the forest
gathering firewood for his grandmother.
"Bring back all you can find," the old woman had said
as she sat knitting a pair of mittens.
"The north wind blows cold, and we must have
a good fire to keep us warm."

All morning the boy worked, picking up sticks,
until his sled was well loaded.
Then a very strange thing happened.
Just as he picked up the last stick
he dropped one of his mittens in the snow.

Now, how a boy could do this
on the coldest day of winter
I'll never know, but that's the way
my grandfather tells the story.

Off he went with his load of wood,
and the mitten was left lying on a snowdrift.

As soon as he was out of sight a little mouse
came scurrying through the woods.
She was very cold, and when she spied the little boy's mitten
with its feathery fur cuff, she popped right in to get warm.
It was just the right size for a tiny mouse.

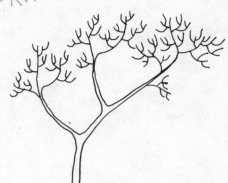

Presently a green frog came hip-hopping over the snow.
"Anybody home?" she asked when she saw the mitten.
"Only me," said the mouse, "and come in quickly
before you freeze."

They had no sooner settled themselves snugly
in the red wool lining when an owl flew down.
"May I join you in that lovely mitten?" he asked.
"If you mind your manners," replied the mouse,
for owls always made her nervous.
"And don't wiggle around too much," added the frog,
"because it's a bit tight in here."

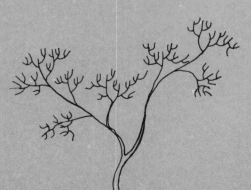

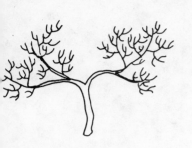

It wasn't long before a rabbit came down the forest path.
"Is there room for me in that nice warm mitten?"
asked the rabbit. "It's awfully cold out here."
"Not much space left," said the mouse
and the frog and the owl.
"But come in. We'll see what we can do."

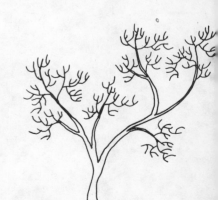

Even before the rabbit had gotten herself tucked in,
a fox trotted up to the mitten,
and after a good deal of trouble
she got herself in along with the others.
The mouse was beginning to think
maybe she shouldn't have been so generous,
but with the bitter wind outside, what else could she do?

And now, as if things weren't bad enough,
the next visitor was a big gray wolf
who wanted to come in, too.
"I don't know how we'll manage it," said the mouse,
"But we'll try."
Everyone moved around a bit, and finally the wolf
was squeezed into the mitten.
It was very crowded by now,
but at least it was warm.

Things had just gotten arranged nicely
when the animals heard a great snorting.
It was a wild boar, and he was very anxious
to get in out of the wind.
"Oh, dear!" cried the mouse, for the mitten
was already beginning to stretch a little.
"We just don't have any more room!"

"I'll be very careful," said the boar.
With that he squinched himself into the mitten
along with the mouse and the frog,
the owl, the rabbit, the fox and the wolf.
I know this is so because my grandfather told me.

But the worst was yet to come,
for who should appear now but a bear!
He was very big and very cold.
"No room! No room!" cried the animals
even before the bear had a chance to speak.

"Nonsense!" said the bear.
"There's always room for one more."
And, without so much as a please or thank you,
he began crawling into the mitten.
He put his paw in first, and the mitten creaked and groaned.
He put his other paw in and one of the seams popped.
Then he took a big breath and pushed himself in.

Now while all this was going on,
along came a little black cricket.
She was very old, and her creaky legs ached with the cold.
When she saw the mitten she said to herself,
"Now that looks like a nice warm place.
I'll just hop over and see if I can squeeze in, too!"

But, ah me, that's all that was needed
to finish off the poor old mitten.
The cricket had no more than put
her first scratchy foot inside when,
with a rip and a snap, the stitches came apart,
the old leather cracked
and the soft red lining split in half,
popping all the animals into the snow!

Well, at this very moment the little boy
discovered that he had only one mitten,
so back he went to see where he might have dropped the other one.
But all he could find were the ripped-apart pieces.
And he thought he saw a little mouse scurrying away
with a bit of red wool perched on her head.
It looked very much like the lining
from the thumb of his missing mitten.

"Oh, well," said the boy as he snuggled his cold hand
inside his coat, "my grandmother will surely have
my new mittens finished by now."

Then he hurried home, with the north wind
nipping at his cheeks.

And my grandfather says he never did know
what *really* happened to his mitten.